PUFF

FREE KICK

Tom Palmer is a football fan and a writer. He never did well at school. But once he got into reading about football – in newspapers, magazines and books – he decided he wanted to be a football writer more than anything. As well as the Football Academy books, he is the author of the Football Detective series, also for Puffin Books.

Tom lives in a Yorkshire town called Todmorden with his wife and daughter. The best stadium he's visited is Real Madrid's Santiago Bernabéu.

Find out more about Tom on his website *tompalmer.co.uk*

TOM PALMER

FOOTBALL ACADEMY

FREE KICK

Illustrated by
Brian Williamson

PUFFIN

PUFFIN BOOKS

Published by the Penguin Group
Penguin Books Ltd, 80 Strand, London WC2R ORL, England
Penguin Group (USA) Inc., 375 Hudson Street, New York, New York 10014, USA
Penguin Group (Canada), 90 Eglinton Avenue East, Suite 700, Toronto, Ontario, Canada M4P 2Y3
(a division of Pearson Penguin Canada Inc.)
Penguin Ireland, 25 St Stephen's Green, Dublin 2, Ireland (a division of Penguin Books Ltd)
Penguin Group (Australia), 250 Camberwell Road, Camberwell, Victoria 3124, Australia
(a division of Pearson Australia Group Pty Ltd)
Penguin Books India Pvt Ltd, 11 Community Centre, Panchsheel Park, New Delhi – 110 017, India
Penguin Group (NZ), 67 Apollo Drive, Rosedale, North Shore 0632, New Zealand
(a division of Pearson New Zealand Ltd)
Penguin Books (South Africa) (Pty) Ltd, 24 Sturdee Avenue, Rosebank,
Johannesburg 2196, South Africa

Penguin Books Ltd, Registered Offices: 80 Strand, London WC2R ORL, England

puffinbooks.com

First published 2009
4

Text copyright © Tom Palmer, 2009
Illustrations copyright © Brian Williamson, 2009
All rights reserved

The moral right of the author and illustrator has been asserted

Set in 14.5/21 pt Baskerville MT
Typeset by Palimpsest Book Production Limited, Grangemouth, Stirlingshire
Made and printed in England by Clays Ltd, St Ives plc

British Library Cataloguing in Publication Data
A CIP catalogue record for this book is available from the British Library

ISBN: 978-0-141-32471-5

www.greenpenguin.co.uk

Penguin Books is committed to a sustainable future
for our business, our readers and our planet.
The book in your hands is made from paper
certified by the Forest Stewardship Council.

For John and Kate Page

Contents

Snow   1

Off to London   8

Sing When You're Winning   17

Bright Lights, Big City   24

Central London   33

Craig in Trouble   40

One-Match Ban   46

West Ham v Chelsea   51

Arsenal v United   58

The Deadly Duo   63

Penalties   68

Like Father, Not Like Son   76

Secret Santas   80

Posh Shopping   84

Thin Ice   90

Red Card   96

The Fan   103

Missing   108

An Announcement   115

Chelsea v United   119

One–Nil   124

Two Minutes   131

Karaoke   138

Father to Son   142

Snow

James sat staring out of his bedroom window – desperate for it to snow.

The weather forecast had been full of warnings all day: twenty centimetres of snow on its way to northern England. But although the clouds were heavy – and the light strange – there was still nothing.

'Are you packed, James?' a loud voice came up the stairs. Dad's voice.

James looked at his bag. It *was* packed, his pair of shin-pads sticking out of one of the side pockets. Three days' clothes. His football boots. A towel. Everything they were told to bring by Steve, the team manager, for a pre-Christmas tournament in London.

The under-twelves team were meeting at the United stadium that morning.

'Yeah, Dad. I'm packed,' James shouted back.

'OK. We'll head off to the stadium in half an hour.'

'All right,' James said. Then he frowned.

James Cunningham had schoolboy terms at United. He was one of the most promising under-twelves central defenders playing for a Premier League club.

His dad had played football for England in the 1980s. He'd scored the winner in a cup final. Then collected the trophy, because he was captain. And most people were sure that

James had a spectacular career as a professional footballer ahead of him.

Like father, like son.

Only *one* person wasn't so sure about that. And that person was James.

Over the last few weeks he'd been questioning everything. And he'd come up with a terrifying answer: he wasn't sure that he really *wanted* to be a professional footballer.

James lay on his bed and tried to

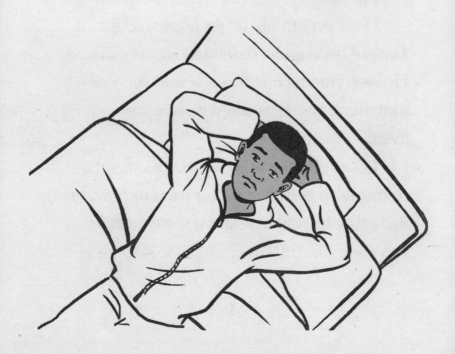

remember the last month. He'd had two bad games for United. And for one game he'd pretended to his dad that he was ill, so he hadn't even played.

It couldn't go on like this, and James knew it.

Something had to happen.

He sat up and stared at his wall. There were posters of his favourite footballers, posters of his favourite bands.

He sighed.

He wasn't thinking about giving up football because he didn't like it. He did. He loved football. It was just that there was something else he wanted to do even more.

James glanced at the football-shaped clock on his bedside table, a present from his dad last Christmas. It said ten past ten. He had twenty minutes before they needed to leave.

He looked outside again. And his heart leaped.

It was *snowing*! It was really snowing. Snowing so hard that he couldn't see the full-sized goal that his dad had had built at the end of their garden.

James left his bedroom and ran downstairs.

'It's snowing!' he shouted. 'Look at it.'

Mum came out of the front room, then Dad from the kitchen with a tea towel in his massive hands.

Mum shook her head, smiling. 'So it is.'

'Don't be so happy about it, James,' Dad said. 'This could threaten the trip. We have to get down the motorway. Two hundred miles to London. I knew we should have set off first thing.'

'Do you think it'll be cancelled?' James asked, aware he'd said it too excitedly – like he *wanted* it to be cancelled.

Dad frowned, as if sensing James's real mood. 'Maybe . . . No, not if we leave now. Let's get going. Make sure no one's for pulling out. I've been looking forward to this trip for weeks.'

Dad grabbed his jacket from the hooks in the hallway. Then he picked up his bag and snatched the car keys from the telephone table.

James realized that his mum was watching him as his dad was getting ready. She was leaning in the doorway looking at him. Her face was half asking a question, half looking worried.

'Are *you* ready to go, James?' she said.

'Yeah,' James said, trying to make his voice sound excited.

'Come on then,' Dad said. 'Before we get snowed in.'

After running upstairs to fetch his bag, James followed his dad out on to the driveway.

Off to London

Dad's silver Range Rover moved effortlessly through the snow. There were already a couple of centimetres settled on the side roads and footpaths by the time they approached the United stadium. And the snowflakes were getting bigger every minute.

James peered out of the window as they drew up by a luxury sixty-seater coach. He noticed Ronan and Connor, both defenders with United, piling huge suitcases into the baggage hold under the bus. The stadium towered over the coach. James could see its huge pipes and panels of steel, with the United crest illuminated above them, still visible through the driving snow.

'They've packed well,' James's dad said, laughing.

'They're flying off to Dublin straight after the tournament,' James said. 'From Heathrow Airport. And Tomasz will be going back to Poland for Christmas.'

'Of course,' Dad said. 'It'll be the day before Christmas Eve when we're done.'

James nodded.

He watched his team-mates being hugged by their parents, then skidding across the snow to get into the coach. It felt good to be here, about to go away with the rest of the team. But he felt confused.

Did he want to be part of this team or not?

James put his hand on the car door handle. He would go. And he'd try to enjoy it, try to forget his doubts.

'Right, lads.'

The full under-twelves squad was on the coach now. Wet coats hung over spare seats at the back. The heaters were blasting hot air around them and snow was sliding down the glass on the outside.

But most of all there was an excitement in the air. It was like electricity, coming from each of the boys.

'We've got fourteen of you lot and four adults,' Steve said. 'The adults are me, then Paul, the under-fourteens coach, James's dad and Mrs Cole, Will's mum. For this trip every adult has as much say as me. If an adult tells you to do something, you do it. OK?'

Fourteen lads nodded.

'We're going to head off now. Try and beat the snow. It's bad here, but it's not snowing in the Midlands. So as long as we get on to the motorway we'll be fine. We –'

'Who are we playing?' a voice shouted, interrupting. It was Craig, the team's left back.

Steve looked irritated for a moment, then his face broke into a smile. 'Arsenal,' he said. 'Then West Ham or Chelsea.'

The bus exploded with noise. Fourteen excited voices shouting – *and* groaning.

Arsenal! They were famously good. This was a challenge the United under-twelves would relish.

Steve clapped his hands firmly. The bus was quiet again.

'Right. Does everyone have their seatbelts on?'

Steve listened to a series of clicks, then nodded.

'Good,' he said. 'Let's get going then.'

The coach driver gunned his engine like a Formula One racer waiting on the grid.

Then they were off.

James was glad that he was sitting next to Chi. He liked Chi. Chi was laid-back. He wasn't one of the more pushy or mouthy members of the team, like Craig, for instance.

Chi was a central midfielder and normally played in front of James, so they

had a good relationship on the pitch – and off it. He would be good company on the drive down.

Chi was fishing around inside a bag. James wondered what he was up to. Then Chi took out two PSP consoles, grinning.

What was this about?

The coach's back wheels skidded dramatically as they turned on to the main road. Several of the team cheered.

'All right, lads. Quiet.' Steve's voice again. 'Let the driver drive.'

Chi took out a sheet of paper and showed it to James.

'We're having a tournament,' he said.

The piece of paper had sixteen names on it. All fourteen boys plus James's dad and Steve. Jake and Connor's names had been ticked; Chi and James's names were next on the list.

'What sort of tournament?' James asked.

'For the trip,' Chi said. 'We're having a *FIFA 10* competition. You know, the football game on PSP? Eight minutes each game. The first round, quarter-finals, semifinals and a final. The winner wins something. I'm not sure what. Steve said he'll sort it once we get to London. Jake's already beaten Connor eleven–nil. Winner goes through to the next round.'

James glanced out at the snow. It was still heavy, but the main roads were clear.

They were going to London. There was no escaping it. So he decided to enjoy himself.

'OK,' James said. 'Can I be England?'

'You can,' Chi said. 'I'm Brazil.'

FIFA 10 First round scores

Connor	0–11	Jake
Chi	3–7	James
Ryan	4–3	Will
Steve	0–2	James's dad
Craig	1–6	Ronan
Ben	2–8	Tomasz
Yunis	0–12	Tony
Sam	5–4	Daniel

Sing When You're Winning

By the time Sam had beaten Daniel five–four in the last game of the first round of *FIFA 10*, the coach was pulling off the motorway.

Craig shouted, 'Are we there?' And everyone laughed when they saw that they were heading into a service station.

The lads were allowed to go where they liked in the service station, as long as they stayed inside.

Steve waited by the door, drinking a cup

of coffee, watching their every move.

The team-mates headed for two places: one lot to the amusement arcade, the other lot to the cafe, watching the next round of the *FIFA 10* tournament.

James was first up against Jake, the team's small but speedy winger.

He knew Jake had a PS3 at home. *And* that he had *FIFA 10*. So this was going to be a hard game.

James wasn't sure he could win.

The cafe was noisy. Food was being served and half the kids were getting themselves a Coke. The more sensible ones were drinking water.

The game between James and Jake was close. James took the lead three times, but Jake pegged him back three times too. James couldn't get his defence right. He wished he'd chosen another formation.

There was a minute to go, so James decided to try to play the way he liked best: quick passing, no time for Jake's players to tackle him. He passed the ball through his defence, up to his midfielders. The clock was running down. In injury time already. So he passed it forward, hoping one of his strikers would get on the end of it. And one did, hoofing it past the keeper.

Four–three.

James had won it in the last seconds.

After watching Ryan's game against James's dad, Jake and James had a look round the amusement arcade. There was loud music. It was the recent *X Factor* winner, a tune everybody knew now.

Craig was in the amusement arcade playing on one of those machines with a shelf of two-pence pieces that you have to try to dislodge by dropping in more coins. But he wasn't doing very well.

Jake noticed him shove the machine.

Immediately an alarm went off. A man in a uniform arrived just as Craig was collecting the coins that he'd 'won'.

Craig was always getting into trouble.

Jake and James watched, frowning.

'He's at it again,' Jake said.

James shrugged.

Jake realized that James hadn't said a word since their *FIFA 10* game.

'I don't mind that you beat me,' Jake said.

James smiled. 'I know. Sorry. I'm miles away.'

'Can I ask you a question?'

'Sure,' James replied.

'Were you really ill for the Bradford game the other week?'

James smiled, then shook his head. Bradford was the game he had missed – on purpose.

'No,' he said.

'Right,' Jake said, then turned to stare at the other end of the service station.

James felt suddenly unhappy. Had Jake turned away and stopped talking to him? Was this the kind of reaction he was going to get if he decided to give up football?

Then Jake turned back to face him.

'I think you need to sort it,' Jake said. 'Can I help you?'

'Sort what?' James asked. Did Jake know what he was thinking?

'Sort whatever it is that's making you sad. You look unhappy.'

James nodded. Maybe Jake was right. Maybe the time *had* come.

FIFA 10 **Quarter-final scores**

James	4–3	Jake
Ryan	4–5	James's dad
Ronan	6–8	Tomasz
Tony	3–6	Sam

Bright Lights, Big City

The coach came off the end of the M1 motorway in London and immediately hit traffic. Slow roads filled with cars and buses and lorries. And roadworks.

Suddenly the coach came to life. The atmosphere had changed. Boys who had been quiet for the whole journey started shouting to each other.

James stared out at the streets. Lots of people were carrying shopping bags, and coloured lights were strung from shop to shop. He saw massive Christmas trees in windows. And everything looked big. This was London, the capital city, where everything was supposed to be big.

Normally James would have been excited by this, like the rest of the team were. He liked coming to London. He liked Christmas. He liked football tournaments. But he couldn't stop himself from worrying.

He closed his eyes, trying to work out his thoughts. But, as he did, he sensed someone near him. He kept his eyes closed. He felt like being alone. Travelling away with everyone wasn't a good thing, not now.

Then he felt an arm come around him.

He opened his eyes.

Dad.

'You've been quiet, James.'

James shrugged. 'Just tired,' he lied.

'Do you know who you've got in the *FIFA 10* semifinal?' Dad asked.

James had forgotten about the tournament. He was miles away. It'd be Ryan: he would be next.

Ryan was the team captain of the under-twelves. Up until a few weeks ago he'd been a bit of a bully. But recently he'd changed – thanks probably to Steve stripping him of the captaincy for a few games. James had grown to like him a lot more. But Ryan was too good at *FIFA 10* for James. He spent hours playing on his PSP at home.

'Ryan?' James said.

'No.' James's dad grinned. 'Me.'

James smiled. 'You beat Ryan?'

'Oh yes,' Dad said.

'He must have let you win,' James said.

'Really?' Dad laughed. 'I suppose you're going to let me win too?'

'Yeah, right.'

'Come on then,' Dad said, narrowing his eyes.

James looked out at the streets again. He thought that they must be in the centre of London. He could see the London Underground tube stations, a tangle of roads, railway bridges.

'Is there time to play?' he said. 'Aren't we nearly there?'

'It'll take a while to get through London,'

Dad said. 'Plenty of time for me to beat you. Then someone else in the final. Then the prize is mine.'

James sat up. 'No way!'

The game was even. James scored with his first attack. But his dad equalized, then took the lead. They knew each other's game too well. James's dad's weakness was that he was always West Ham. James was United. That gave him the upper hand, because United were better than West Ham on *FIFA 10*.

But his dad was *so* competitive. His players went flying into tackles and he never gave up possession.

With seconds to go it was two–two. Then James's dad picked up the ball and shot from the halfway line. The ball bounced once in front of James's keeper. The keeper jumped to catch it, but it slipped through his fingers. And fell into the net.

A massive cheer went up behind James. He looked round. Half the lads were watching the game over his shoulder.

'Beaten by your old man,' Craig said, shaking his head. 'Pathetic, James. Pathetic.'

James shook his dad's hand, trying to be sportsmanlike, but underneath he felt really angry. More with Craig than his dad.

James's dad looked over to Tomasz, who had also made it to the final.

'I'll have to beat you later, Tomasz,' he said. 'We're nearly there.'

Then there was a shout: 'Sit DOWN!' Steve had spotted some of the lads out of their seats.

As the boys got back to their seats the coach turned into a large square and they fell silent. They had all seen it at the same time: a giant clock tower.

'Big Ben!' shouted Jake.

'I saw it when I was down in London to visit my dad,' Craig said quickly and equally loudly. 'That's the Houses of Parliament. And the Ouse is over there.'

'The Ouse?' Steve said. 'Are you sure, Craig?'

'Yeah!' But Craig *didn't* sound sure.

'The Thames,' Yunis said. 'The Ouse is the river in York.'

Suddenly several people were laughing.

'And that's the moon,' Ryan was saying, trying to speak in Craig's voice. 'And behind it, that's the Pacific Ocean.'

More laughter.

But Craig said nothing. He just scowled at Ryan.

James watched him. And he had a strong feeling that Craig was going to be trouble on this trip – big trouble.

FIFA 10 Semifinal scores

James	2–3	James's dad
Tomasz	5–1	Sam

Central London

The coach pulled up on a very busy street, next to a towering building that said 'Student Accommodation' over the doorway. This was where they were going to stay for the next three nights.

Right in the centre of London.

It was after 6 p.m., but the streets were still packed with shoppers. There was noise from voices and cars – a general rumble that never stopped.

There was a big clothes shop opposite the student accommodation.

'Look at all those people in there,' Jake said.

James nodded. It *was* packed. There were queues at all the tills.

There was also a huge Starbucks cafe. Two floors of people drinking teas and coffees.

'It'd be really quiet in the centre of town at home by this time,' James said.

'I know,' Jake replied. 'Is London always like this?'

'I suppose so,' James said. He knew: he'd come to the capital a lot with his dad.

'Don't you like it?'

'It's OK,' James said.

Jake smiled. 'Part of me wishes we were at home. All the snow and that.'

James nodded.

'But playing Arsenal tomorrow,' Jake said. 'That's going to be amazing.'

James nodded again. He tried to smile too. He didn't want Jake to think he wasn't as excited as he was.

Once they were inside the student accommodation building, Steve lined everyone up in what looked like a canteen. Fourteen lads and four adults.

James looked around him. He saw loads

of tables and chairs and a huge noticeboard with scraps of paper pinned all over it. Along the side of the canteen were large windows, all with metal grilles protecting them from the street.

It looked like a cross between a school and a prison.

'Right, lads. This is where we're staying. These rooms belong to students in term time, but the university has cleared them so we can use them.'

'Have they all gone?' Sam asked.

'Who?'

'The students?'

James heard Craig snigger.

'Yes, Sam, they're all home with their parents now, I expect.' Steve paused. 'Before we go up to the bedrooms,' he said, 'I want to make one thing clear. Once you're in your rooms, you need to stay there. I don't want to

find you exploring the rest of the building.
I want to know where you are all the time.
Tomorrow we'll be out for most of the day
and after *that* we'll have a chance to do a bit
of exploring.' Steve pointed out to the street.
'But tonight I want you to eat here in an
hour. Then bed. Got it?'

Several lads nodded.

'After you've finished, Will's mum will be
coming round to check you're all settled in.
If there is *any* messing, there are two things
I can do,' Steve said. 'One: I can drop you
from a game. Two: I can send you home.
Understand?'

More nods.

'I don't want to be overdramatic and I do want us to have a great time,' Steve added. 'But I will do both those things, if necessary.'

James was sharing a room with Jake. He was pleased. Jake was easy-going, like Chi. If he had to stay with someone like Craig it'd be a nightmare.

After they'd eaten in the canteen, James and Jake went back up to their room,

following Craig and Sam, who had sprinted up ahead of them.

Once they were settled, Will's mum came in.

'OK, boys?' she said gently.

'Yes, thanks,' the two boys said at once.

'Remember, no messing about and lights out in thirty minutes,' she said, still in a kind voice.

And James remembered what Steve had said. He knew that if anyone *did* mess about, Steve would be down on them like a ton of bricks.

Craig in Trouble

The room had two single beds and a sink by the door. Apart from a bit of cupboard space, that was it. James was lying on one of the beds, doing nothing. He was thinking about the match the next day and how he didn't feel as up for it as he should.

Jake was staring out of the window. He saw that the city was still really busy. Their room was three floors up and there was a lot to watch: groups of men and women walking slowly, calling out to each other, going in and out of pubs and restaurants; people rushing into a tube station; cars beeping at each other.

And the thing Jake noticed most of all: the air was badly polluted. He could taste exhaust fumes even up on the third floor.

Jake craned his neck to look a bit further out. He could just see into a square along the next road. A strange pale light was coming from it, and music.

Something was going on. It wasn't like the other streets.

'What do you reckon that is?' Jake asked.

James jumped off the bed and peered out. He said nothing for a few seconds, then squinted. 'It's an ice rink. Look –' James pointed – 'there's people coming away with skates.'

Jake looked again.

'You're right. Do you reckon they'll let us

go tomorrow night?' he said in an excited
voice.

'I dunno. They'll be worried we'll do our
ankles, I reckon,' James said, lying down on
the bed again. 'They won't want us getting
injured.'

'True,' Jake agreed. Then he gazed back
down at the street. 'James?' he said, after a
minute. 'Are you happy at United?'

'What?'

'I just feel like you're not enjoying it. The
last few weeks.'

James didn't know what to say. Had Jake uncovered his secret? Was it so obvious that James was having doubts? How could people tell? Now he was going to have to tell him. Or at least say something.

'I . . . I'm not sure,' James said.

'How do you mean?' asked Jake, turning to glance out of the window again.

James didn't know what to say in response to Jake. He was trying to put the right words together when Jake shouted.

'James!'

'Yeah?'

'Is that Craig?'

'What?'

James got up again and came over to the window. He looked down. 'It is,' he said. 'What's he up to?'

Craig was standing outside the door of the student accommodation block, several people walking past him. And a policeman was talking to him.

James called his dad on his mobile. He didn't need to think twice.

'Craig's outside the main door,' James said quickly, 'and the police are with him.'

Jake and James watched the rest from their window above. James's dad – and Steve – were outside in seconds. Steve went up to the policeman and Craig.

The policeman was talking quickly to

Steve. He looked angry. They saw Steve
nodding, then shaking the policeman's hand.
Then everyone moved out of view, so neither
Jake nor James could see what was going on.

They heard the door slam.

And the city carried on making its noises.
Everything was back to normal.

'What was that all about?' Jake asked.

'I dunno,' James replied. 'But I reckon
Craig's getting a right telling-off now.'

One-Match Ban

There was a strange silence at breakfast the next morning.

Something had happened overnight, but nobody knew quite what.

Steve and James's dad were chatting with Will's mum. The adults were making sure all the boys had what they wanted to eat. *And* that they took their empty plates and mugs to the right place.

Nobody dared ask anyone else what had happened.

James looked over at Craig a couple of times, but Craig was just looking at his bowl, moving his cereal around with a spoon, not eating it.

'Right, lads,' Steve said.

Nobody even smiled when he said this. It had become a joke that Steve always started saying things with 'Right, lads'. But today it wasn't funny.

'Last night I told you all to stay in the building,' Steve continued. 'I'd like to thank the eleven of you that did.'

None of the boys' eyes moved from Steve.

'But last night three of you – Craig, Sam and Daniel – did *not*. Those three were found *outside* the main door in what could have been a very serious situation. They're all on a final warning. And they're all dropped from today's game.'

A murmur went round the room.

'It's my responsibility to keep you safe on this trip,' Steve went on. 'We are in London, one of the biggest and therefore potentially most dangerous cities in the world. I've said all I'm going to say. Any more trouble and the same punishments apply.'

Steve stood up, took his empty dishes to stack for washing and left the room.

James looked at his dad, but his dad was still talking to Will's mum.

Then James saw Craig looking at him. There was no expression on Craig's face. But it made James wonder if Craig knew that it was him who had told the adults he was out on the street last night.

Half an hour later the coach was waiting for them outside the accommodation block.

James sat behind Jake and Yunis. Yunis was the team's leading scorer, a fast striker who was quiet off the pitch but strong on it.

James was still feeling uneasy. They were going to play the tournament at West Ham's training ground. His dad's old club.

Jake was bouncing around in his seat. 'Do you think they'll be good?' he asked.

'Course,' Yunis said. 'They're Arsenal players, so they must be. And their attack is supposed to be amazing.'

'Well, James can handle them,' Jake said, turning round. 'Can't you, James?'

James nodded.

'*You're* quiet,' said Yunis.

'Yeah.' James smiled. 'I just get nervous going to West Ham. Everyone goes mad over Dad – and they make a big fuss of me too.'

Yunis nodded, but said nothing.

Jake looked at James, wishing he'd talked to him more about how he was feeling the night before, when they'd been interrupted by Craig outside on the street.

He felt like James had something to say.

West Ham v Chelsea

West Ham's training facilities were a bit like United's: a block of buildings clustered together; several large pitches; a lot of fancy first-team cars in the car park.

James could see that his dad was waiting for him so that they could get off the coach together. Father and son.

And as soon as they were outside, the former West Ham player was being called out to. Every other man in a tracksuit wanted to come up and shake his hand.

'Cyril! How's it going?'

'Cyril! Have you come back for a game?'

'Cyril! How's life in the frozen north?'

And everyone was laughing. They were happy to see the man who had lifted the cup for them in the 1980s. The man who had scored the winning goal.

Then the focus turned on James, who had

been thinking how strange it was to hear his dad called by his first name. Especially as it was such a *weird* name.

'Your lad's getting big now, Cyril. He's looking good. Still at United, son?'

'Yes,' James said.

'It's going OK?'

'Great,' James said.

'You're going to be pulling on an England shirt one day, son. Just like your dad. I can tell.'

Then there was more laughter.

Jake watched James getting all the attention but looking gloomy. What *had* James been trying to tell him last night?

'Right, lads,' Steve said, calling everyone together. 'Come on. Let's get into the dressing rooms. I want us to have a short training session before we watch the West Ham–Chelsea game.'

*

All fourteen players trained on the pitch nearest to the dressing rooms. It was just gentle running and a bit of ball control. They had a match in three hours, so they didn't want to use up too much energy. Steve had asked the three banned players – Craig and Sam and Daniel – to train too, even though they wouldn't play later.

But Jake noticed that none of them were trying. Jake was surprised. If he'd been caught doing something wrong, he'd be doing his best to be good, not making it worse.

At one point, when Steve had gone back into the dressing rooms, Jake noticed Ryan go over to them. They talked for a while. Then Craig seemed to shout at Ryan, waving his arms about. Then Ryan walked away, shaking his head.

What's the matter with Craig? Jake wondered. *Why is he being so stupid?*

*

After they had trained they went to watch the
first game in the tournament.

West Ham had to play Chelsea, then it
was Arsenal against United. The winners
would play each other the following day for
the trophy: the Christmas Cup. There would
also be a losers' final.

James and Jake stood with Connor and

Ronan to watch the West Ham–Chelsea game. It was ten minutes in.

'They're good,' Ronan said.

'They are,' Connor agreed.

'I reckon we could beat West Ham,' Jake said. 'But Chelsea look amazing. They like to get lots of crosses into the box early, don't they, James?'

James shrugged his shoulders. 'Suppose,' he said.

'Steve thinks we need to play direct stuff against them,' Connor said.

'Yeah?' Jake asked.

'He said we need to be physical. Put them off a bit.'

Jake smiled. He liked Steve and how he was always thinking of ways to stop the other team. That was the difference between playing for a village team and a Premier League under-twelves team.

But if they were to play either of these teams, they had to beat Arsenal. And that was going to be the hardest game they'd had all season.

Arsenal v United

'This is a good team we're going to be playing,' Steve said quietly. 'And they've got a lot of fans.'

United were having their team talk on the pitch, in a huddle, twenty metres from the Arsenal players having their team talk.

Around the pitch there were at least two hundred people watching. They were families of the players and fans of the three London clubs.

'Don't be put off,' Steve went on. 'We can

win this. Arsenal pass it like the men's team. And they're strong and fit. But here's what I want you to do . . .'

On the pitch everyone had been given a job and some rules on how to play against Arsenal. The first rule was play deep, not to let the Arsenal players get behind them. Keep it very tight, so they had no room to pass in.

James was based in the centre of defence, as usual. And – also like usual recently – he felt only half interested in the game. In the last month he'd made some bad mistakes on the pitch because he wasn't as up for it as he used to be. Something was missing.

But they were at West Ham, his dad's old club. He knew his dad would be wanting him to do his best in front of all his friends.

So he put his confused thoughts to the

back of his mind. He'd do this. Then tonight
he would think. Think hard.

Arsenal scored their first goal within three
minutes.

Their players were moving so quickly –
and passing the ball so perfectly – it was
impossible to get near them.

James did everything he could to get to
the ball. He made two tackles before it ran

loose and the Arsenal star player – Theo Bingley – was on to it. He collected the ball effortlessly and slotted it home.

One–nil.

After that, James, Ryan and Chi worked hard to get the United team to keep the ball more. And when Arsenal attacked, United managed to hold them off, packing the midfield, then the defence. But it was hard. If the United back line had lost their concentration for a second they would have conceded again.

At half-time it was still one–nil. And Steve was delighted.

'Great stuff. You're doing just what I asked. Defenders: excellent. James especially. Your heads could have dropped when the goal went in, but they didn't. Great stuff.'

Steve paused and looked over at the Arsenal team.

'The second half is about stamina,' he said. 'They look like they might get tired doing all this work. If we can hold them off, we only need to hit them on the break once. Jake? Yunis? I want you to be on the look-out for the opening. Everyone else, play deep. I want forty-five minutes more out of you. Remember, there are no subs for us. But I know you eleven can get a result here.'

The Deadly Duo

It was hard going. With ten minutes left to play, United had kept the score to one–nil. But it wasn't good enough. They needed one goal. At least.

Ryan was talking to everyone, being a great captain.

'Come on. Keep it up!' he shouted. 'You're doing brilliant. Jake? Yunis? Be ready.'

And, five minutes later, Jake saw Ryan collect the ball after an Arsenal attack had broken down. Instinctively Jake ran wide up the pitch. He saw Yunis move up level with the Arsenal defenders at the same time.

Then Ryan fired the ball out to Jake. Jake took it in his stride and ran. This was great. They'd been defending for eighty-five minutes and he'd barely had a chance to use the ball. He moved wide to the edge of the area. Two big Arsenal defenders were ready to close him down.

But they weren't ready for what he did next. Without looking up, Jake crossed the ball high to the near post. How many times this season had he looked across to see Yunis there, ready to score?

Loads.

So this time he didn't even look up.

After he crossed the ball he fell over, his thigh cramping painfully. But he managed to look up to see what had happened.

The Arsenal keeper was on his back. The ball was in the net.

The Deadly Duo had struck again and Yunis was sprinting towards Jake, grinning.

Arsenal 1 United 1.

Jake raised his arms and shouted.

Six minutes later the referee blew his whistle. One–one was the final score.

James felt OK. He'd had a good game and his dad looked happy. He noticed that

Ryan had been talking to Steve, but now
Ryan was running towards the players.

Jake had gone down on to the pitch,
holding his thigh. It was still painful and he
dreaded playing extra time.

Ryan stopped as he reached the ten lads.
'Penalties,' he said.

'I thought it was extra time,' Chi pointed
out.

'No, it's penalties. Steve and the Arsenal
manager have agreed it. What with the match

tomorrow too. Who wants it?' Ryan asked. 'Step forward if you do. I need five.'

Yunis and Will stepped forward straight away, then Ben. Ryan joined them.

Chi shook his head. So did most of the others.

Jake said, 'I can't. My leg. I would . . .'

Ryan nodded. 'One more,' he said.

Then James stepped forward. 'I'll do it.'

Penalties

Both teams gathered near the centre of the pitch, Arsenal to the left of the centre circle, United to the right.

The referee called the captains over and tossed a coin. Ryan called out heads and it *was* heads.

'We'll go second,' Ryan said, patting the United keeper, Tomasz, on the back. Tomasz was Polish and had been with the team less than two years, but he was a great keeper –

and had already proved that he could save
penalties this season.

But when the first Arsenal player stepped
up to shoot, Tomasz dived left. The ball went
right.

Arsenal 1 United 0.

Then Will – Yunis's striking partner –
placed the ball on the spot. He eyed the
Arsenal keeper, who was huge for his age – as
big as a grown man.

Will hit the ball to the right. The keeper
went to the right too, palming the ball round
the post.

Arsenal 1 United 0. Still.

As Will came back to the team, Ryan put
his arm round him. 'Don't worry,' he said.
'It's hard.'

Then the second Arsenal player scored
his penalty.

Arsenal 2 United 0.

It wasn't looking good.

Jake wished he could take a penalty, but his leg was still cramping. He had it stretched out, with Chi holding his foot to help relieve the pain.

Then Yunis stepped up and Jake smiled. He knew Yunis would score.

And he did.

Arsenal 2 United 1.

Ryan went over to Tomasz and whispered something in his ear. Tomasz grinned, then nodded.

The third Arsenal player took the ball and placed it on the spot.

Then Tomasz smiled at him.

Ryan had talked to Tomasz about the final. If they won this shoot-out, they'd be playing Chelsea to win the Christmas Cup. And they'd be the first team from outside London to do it, according to Steve. That was what he'd told Tomasz, to motivate him.

The Arsenal player drove the ball straight down the middle. Tomasz stood still and caught it.

Arsenal 2 United 1.

Ryan went up to Ben and James. He repeated what he'd said to Tomasz. They could reach the final, be the first northern team to win this cup.

Ben stepped up – and scored. Two–two.

But the next Arsenal player scored too. Three–two.

Then Ryan scored. It was three–three.

There were two players left to shoot: the Arsenal striker who had come on as a substitute, and James.

The Arsenal striker swaggered up to the ball. He looked like he'd already scored. He smirked at Tomasz and Tomasz smiled back.

Then – without taking a run-up – the striker stroked the ball to the far-left corner of the goal. Tomasz leaped, his legs propelling his long arms to tip the ball on to the post.

The ball came back into play and the Arsenal striker thrashed it into the net.

But the referee shook his head.

No goal, no rebounds – and everyone knew it.

Ryan jumped into the air and ran to Tomasz, putting his arm round his back. If

United scored their last penalty they'd be in the final to play Chelsea.

Jake was pleased with what he saw. Ryan was being a really good captain now. In the past he'd not been so good, but now he was a real leader. It was great to see him being so friendly with Tomasz. Only weeks ago they'd hated each other.

James picked up the ball. *I'm going to score,*

he said to himself. *I'm not going to worry about being a United player. I am just going to put the ball on the spot – and score.*

He put the ball down. Stepped back. Glanced to the left of the goal. Took two steps. And hammered the ball as hard as he could high into the centre of the net.

The keeper dived left.

The ball hit the net so hard a shower of rain came down off the crossbar, soaking the Arsenal keeper.

Arsenal 3 United 4.

United were in the final.

Wednesday 21 December
Arsenal 1 United 1
United win 4–3 on penalties
Goals: Yunis
Penalties: Yunis, Ben, Ryan, James
Bookings: none

Under-twelves manager's marks out of ten for each player:

Tomasz	9
Connor	7
James	9
Ryan	9
Ronan	7
Chi	7
Tony	7
Jake	9
Yunis	9
Will	7
Ben	8

Like Father,
Not Like Son

When James came out of the
dressing room, he saw his dad
was surrounded by his old friends
again together with the West Ham coaches –
and staff from Chelsea and Arsenal.

James was used to this. Whenever they
went anywhere – especially to do with
football – his dad would get lots of
handshakes and pats on the back. It even
happened in the supermarket sometimes, or
in the town centre. People would stare and

point. Sometimes they would come up to
him, telling him that they saw him play
in 1983 and how he'd made them really
happy, going on and on about his headed
goal in the cup final when he'd won it for
West Ham.

James was OK with this, mostly because
he was used to it. But he was uncomfortable
when the attention turned on him. And he
hated it when people started telling him
things like he was going to be an England
international just like his dad.

So he wasn't happy with what happened
next.

First a cheer went up. Then they all
started clapping. Five grown men were
applauding James, including his dad.

James tried to smile.

'Here comes England's next world-cup-
winning captain,' one man said. James sort

of recognized him. He looked like a player he'd seen photos of with his dad at West Ham.

'We hope so. Don't we?' James's dad said.

'He'll be lifting a trophy like you did, Cyril. I can see it.'

James just smiled. He didn't want to actually say yes.

'That was a great performance, son,' another man said. James didn't recognize him. 'You held that defence together superbly. I don't think anyone's ever kept Arsenal down to just one. You and that captain of yours were heroes.'

'Thank you,' James said, knowing his dad was watching him.

'So how are you enjoying it at United?' the man said.

'Great, thanks,' James said.

But inside he was starting to feel angry

and all his anger was aimed at his dad. Why couldn't his dad see that he hated this? Why couldn't his dad stop them going on at him?

'We're really happy with United,' his dad said. 'The coaching is right and so is the balance between school and football. Obviously he'll have to put more in when he's fifteen and sixteen to get a full contract. But now it's just right.'

James smiled on the outside, gazing across at the team bus. He wished he was on it, listening to music. Very loud music.

Why did his dad not know him at all?

Why did he think he was going to do exactly what he had done?

Why did he think the best thing in the world was being a footballer?

Secret Santas

Steve was in a good mood on the coach leaving West Ham. He was wearing a Santa hat and grinning.

'Right, lads.'

The boys burst out laughing.

'What?' Steve said, half smiling. 'Anyway. That was great today. I am *so* proud of you. What a result! You beat one of the best under-twelves teams in Europe. I couldn't be happier.'

Steve then picked up a bucket from one of the front seats.

'This,' he said, 'is the Secret Santa bucket. In each envelope there is a tenner and the name of one of us. It could be one of the lads – or one of us adults. We're off Christmas shopping now and I want you to choose a ten-pound present for whoever's name you get in the draw. OK?'

The whole team cheered.

Steve started to hand out the envelopes.

Connor opened his envelope first. 'I got Ronan!' he shouted.

Steve sighed. 'Connor? Do you understand what secret means? It's meant to be a *secret* who the present is from.'

Connor blushed deep red. 'Sorry, Steve.'

Steve carried on giving out envelopes.

Jake was delighted to get Ryan. He'd come to like him recently. He wanted to get him something really good.

Yunis got Steve.

Ryan got Tomasz.

And James knew who he was going to get before he opened it, he just had a feeling. And he was right. His dad. Typical.

Since all the attention he'd got after the game, James had been feeling bad. Yes, he'd scored. Yes, he'd played well. But it didn't change anything. In fact, he was even more determined now to give up football after all the praise he'd had. Too many people had his life planned out for him and he wanted to plan it himself.

He'd made up his mind.

Posh Shopping

They had to get the presents in a department store. Just the one shop, so there was no chance of getting lost on the streets.

'Right, lads. You've got half an hour to choose a present and buy it. Do *not* leave the store. I will be here by the main doors the whole time. So if you need me, you know where I am.'

The department store was big. And posh. The Christmas decorations were huge, massive silver and gold and red tinsel stars hanging down. Strings of lights were cascading like waterfalls.

Jake and Yunis raced off to get their presents together.

'Who've you got?' Yunis asked.

'You,' replied Jake.

'Really?' Yunis said. 'What are you going to get me?'

'Some aftershave,' Jake said, grinning.

'What? No way,' Yunis said. Then he saw Jake smiling. 'Who have you really got?'

'Ryan.'

'I've got Steve,' said Yunis.

'Brilliant. What are you going to get him?'

'Some carpet slippers? A pipe? A walking stick?'

Yunis and Jake laughed as they headed up an escalator.

As they did, they looked down and saw

Craig. He was trying to walk *up* the escalator that was going *downwards*. A security guard was watching him, talking into his radio.

'What's he up to now?' Yunis said to Jake.

Jake shrugged. 'Who knows?'

'Let's get those presents,' Yunis said, turning to go upwards.

James sat alone at the back of the coach, brooding. He'd not got his dad a present. The ten-pound note was still in its envelope, stuffed in his back pocket.

He was unhappy. Unsettled. Un-everything.

The thought of spending all evening with the rest of the team depressed him. He wanted to be alone, to think.

He stared out of the window as the coach moved off. Shops and more shops. Christmas trees. And the ice rink – just round the corner from their accommodation.

Three other lads were sitting near the back of the bus. They'd been with each other for most of the day. Craig, Daniel and Sam. They hadn't noticed James two seats behind them.

'Did you see that?' Craig asked.

'What?'

'The ice rink?'

'Yeah, I wish we could –' Daniel began to say. But Craig interrupted him.

'Let's then,' Craig said. 'After they've all gone to bed. It was easy to get out last night. They'll never think that we'd try it again. How about it?'

'OK,' said Daniel.

Sam was less sure. 'I can't risk it. Steve will go nuts.'

'He won't find out,' Craig said.

'What if he does?' Sam insisted. 'I can't.'

'Suit yourself,' Craig said.

Then James was standing over him. Craig looked shocked and stared at James. James knew what he was thinking: that James had called his dad last night to get Craig into trouble.

For a few seconds nobody said anything.

'I suppose you're going to split on us, James,' Craig said. 'Again.'

'Not if you let me come with you,' replied James.

At first Craig looked surprised, as if he didn't believe James. Then a smile crept across his face.

'You're on,' he said.

Thin Ice

Ryan was too excited to sleep. He was going over the game in his mind: the defending he'd done with James, the penalty shoot-out. He wondered if he'd said the right things to the other players and if his firing them up had worked or not.

Then he heard a noise.

Running footsteps in the corridor.

Ryan waited for a few seconds, then opened his door a crack.

He saw three figures, all in coats. They

were rushing, going down the stairs.

At first he thought it could be some of the adults, heading off for a pint. But the figures were too small. It was either three of his team-mates or three strangers.

Ryan pulled on his jeans and a T-shirt. He was captain of this team and he had to see what was going on. He had his suspicions about who he was about to follow. There was something about the figure in the middle that reminded him of someone.

By the time he got down to the entrance hall by the canteen the main door had closed. Ryan breathed in. What now?

Tell Steve?

Follow them and get them to come back?

Do nothing?

Ryan was feeling good about being team captain and if he could stop some of his players doing something stupid he'd do it –

before they got into any more trouble with
Steve.

Ryan opened the door to the street.
There was a piece of card stuck to the lock.
To keep it open, he realized. Whoever had
gone out was expecting to come back in.

Ryan had to look up and down the street
to see them. It took a few seconds, but there
they were. Craig, definitely. Daniel, he
thought too. And the other figure looked
like James, but Ryan knew it couldn't be him.
James wouldn't be so stupid as to do what
Steve had told them *not* to do.

Ryan followed quickly. He wanted to get to them as soon as he could. Make them stop, make them see sense.

But it was hard. There were still a lot of people about. Most of them were going to or coming away from what looked like the ice rink Ryan had seen from the coach earlier. The roads were busy and noisy. It was hard to cross any of them. And people didn't move out of the way to let Ryan get by. They seemed happier to walk into him or barge him out of the way.

It wasn't until he reached the rink that he caught up with the others. They were standing by the entrance under a massive Christmas tree. Craig was going through his pockets.

Looking for money, Ryan assumed. Then James caught his eye.

Ryan went over quickly. He saw James's face fall.

'What are you doing?' Ryan said.

'Come to join us?' Craig said. 'It'll be a laugh.'

They were standing in a circle now: Ryan, Craig, Daniel, James.

But James hadn't registered that Ryan was there at all. He was staring over Ryan's shoulder, still looking sad – or scared.

Ryan looked behind him, then back at James.

'What are you looking at?' Ryan asked.

'You were followed,' James said in a low voice.

Ryan looked round, puzzled, expecting trouble.

Then he saw Steve. And Paul. And James's dad. All three with faces like thunder.

Red Card

'What's this?'

Steve was the only one to have spoken, and in a quiet voice. Nobody was used to Steve talking in a quiet voice.

'An ice rink,' Craig said.

James couldn't believe Craig. What *was* the matter with him? He was breaking rules, answering back, like he couldn't care less. Craig might do that with teachers. What

could they do? But with Steve? The United
coach? It was madness.

James looked at his dad. His dad
appeared calm too. He was just looking at
James with a question in his eyes.

'Ryan?' Steve said, turning to his team
captain.

James broke in. 'Ryan has only just got
here. He was trying to get us to come back.
He's nothing to do with this.'

Ryan looked at James. His plan to save his

team-mates from getting into any more trouble had failed.

'Is that right, Ryan?' Steve asked.

Ryan nodded.

'Right, you go back to the rooms with Paul. Is that OK, Paul?'

Paul nodded and headed off back the way they'd come, with Ryan alongside him.

'Anything else to say?' Steve asked. His voice was getting louder. He looked at the three boys in front of him.

Nobody spoke.

'Right. Craig, Daniel. Come back with me. You're both getting the train home in the morning.'

Craig and Daniel said nothing. James could see they were trying to look like they weren't bothered, but he could tell they were. They knew they'd made a huge mistake.

'Cyril. James is out of the team tomorrow.

I expect you'd like to walk back with your son alone?'

'I would,' James's dad said.

Steve set off back to the accommodation. Craig and Daniel followed behind, without him having to ask them to.

'What's going on?' James's dad said.

He asked this as if he was expecting a reasonable explanation, that James had been with Ryan trying to stop the others breaking such a big rule.

They were walking back now, the ice rink and its noise and music fading behind them.

'I was with Craig and Daniel,' James said.

'But why? I don't understand.'

'I was going ice-skating.'

James's dad stopped walking. 'What?'

'I wanted to get out. Be on my own.'

'So you went ice-skating with Craig?'
Dad's voice was louder now.

James noticed a couple of older girls
looking over.

He wasn't sure what to say. But one thing
he wanted was to be honest. And more than
that, he wanted this to be the moment he told
his dad he didn't really want to be a footballer.

But how could he get the words out?

'I don't understand,' Dad said again. 'It's
so unlike you.'

'What am I like?' James snapped.

'What do you mean?' Dad replied.

'What am I like?' James repeated. 'Do you know what I'm really like?'

James could feel himself becoming more and more angry. And he realized this was good. If he got really angry he might be able to spit it out: tell his dad how he actually felt.

'I think I know what you're like,' Dad said, calm again now. 'You're hard-working. You're respectful. You're a good lad. I thought you'd had a good day.'

'*Not* a good day,' James said. He could feel tears coming into his eyes, but he held them back.

'What?'

'Not good. I hated it.'

James's dad stopped. 'Hated what?'

'All of it.'

'But . . .'

James wanted to push his dad, find a way
of getting him to understand. But all he could
say was 'what', over and over again. It was
driving James mad.

So he just said it.

'I don't want to be a footballer, Dad.
I want to give it up.' Then he looked at his
dad's face, waiting for a reaction.

The Fan

Dad took James to a cafe rather than go straight back to the student accommodation.

'I don't understand,' Dad said when they were sitting down. He seemed really sad.

'I don't want to play any more,' James said. 'Not training two days a week. Then playing. I want to –'

'Have I pushed you too hard?' Dad interrupted. 'I thought you enjoyed it. All this.'

'I do, but . . .'

'So why? You always said you were happy with the football.'

James was finding it hard to speak. His dad kept interrupting and his voice was getting louder. People were starting to look over.

James could see in his dad's eyes that he was struggling, but he couldn't be sure if it was anger or disappointment. Or both.

James wanted to tell him the truth, the reason. About the other thing he wanted to do. But he was interrupted again.

'Think of all the time we've put into this,' Dad said. 'All the money.'

And then a man was standing beside them. He was tall with short brown hair, maybe thirty or forty years old, and carrying a guitar. James noticed a small West Ham badge on his guitar case.

'Excuse me? Am I interrupting? My name's Jim.'

James's dad turned and smiled. 'No, not at all,' he said. And he was wearing the face he wore when he spoke to fans. A smile. A nodding head. It was a face James knew well.

James wanted to shout at the man, to tell him to go away.

Dad talked to him. The fan wanted to chat about the cup final, the famous goal, how grateful he was. And could he have Cyril's autograph?

James watched the other people in the cafe. They all seemed so excited, all talking. Talking, talking, talking.

James wished he was at home in his room with his music on full blast and his eyes closed.

When the man had gone, Dad looked at James.

'Sorry,' he said. 'What were we saying?'

'That says it all, Dad,' James said.

'What?'

'That. I don't want that.' James gestured at the fan who was leaving the cafe.

Dad looked at the man and turned back to James. Then he nodded. 'I see. So what *do* you want?' His voice was quiet.

James shrugged. He was feeling confused.

He didn't know what to say. The words were stuck.

Dad stood up. 'Right,' he said. 'Let's go. I can't deal with any more of this tonight.'

James stood up too and followed his dad back.

Neither of them spoke.

Missing

Breakfast was even weirder on the second morning than it had been the first.

Again, few people were speaking.

Jake was sitting next to Yunis. He leaned over to James. 'Where's Craig and Daniel?' he asked.

'They've gone,' James said, deadpan. There was no feeling in his voice.

Jake wondered what had happened to

him the night before. He'd come in late, but said nothing.

'What?' Yunis cut in.

'Steve sent them home,' James answered. 'He'll tell us all about it, I'm sure.'

Steve had just come into the canteen. He stood and looked at the boys from the doorway. James's dad came in behind him, walked to a table and sat down.

'More news,' Steve said to the room. And then he turned to look at James. James wasn't sure, but he thought Steve was trying to smile at him. Then again, it could have been a frown.

'Last night,' Steve went on, 'some of the squad were caught outside again. Craig and Daniel have been sent home. They're on their way to King's Cross station with Paul now.'

Silence. No one dared say a word.

Steve paused. 'That's it. Let me eat my

breakfast then I'll tell you what's happening the rest of today.'

Everyone went back to their cereal and toast. Some conversations started up, but only quietly.

James stared at his dad. What was going on? Surely Steve should have announced that James was dropped from the game? He ran through the conversations he'd had with his dad the night before.

James hadn't expected his dad to be angry. He didn't normally get angry.

He saw his dad gesture with his head that James should come over to talk to him.

James pushed his chair away and walked to his dad. They sat alone at a table.

'I talked to Steve last night,' Dad said.

James nodded. What had they talked about? Had he pulled in a favour? Don't drop James because he's my boy, the son of an England international? Something like that?

'Go on,' James said, still unsure how his dad felt about him today.

'I told him you wanted to pack it in,' Dad said.

James swallowed. Now it was real. Now he couldn't go back. He said nothing.

Neither did his dad.

'Right,' James said eventually.

'I won't say I'm not disappointed, James . . .'

James looked down at his hands. This was the last thing he wanted to hear.

'But,' Dad went on, 'I talked to your mum on the phone late last night and if that's how you feel, then that's how you feel. I'm not going to force you to do anything you don't want to do.'

This was his answer. It was agreed. Mum and Dad had talked about it. James felt half

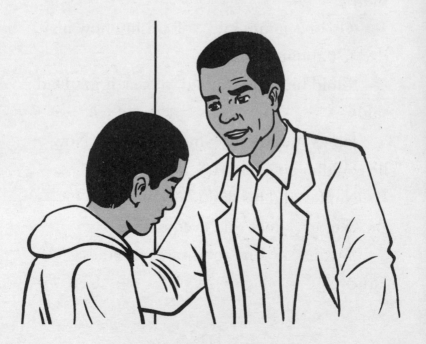

scared of what he'd done. And half freed by
it.

'Thanks, Dad,' he muttered.

'So, James, what do you want to do so
much?'

'Well, er . . .' James hesitated. He was
dying to tell his dad, but somehow it still
wouldn't come out. Again, there was
something in his dad's voice. That
disappointment. He wasn't sure how his dad
would react. He might laugh at him and
think he was stupid.

'Steve asked me to try and change your
mind,' Dad said, 'but I said I wouldn't.'

James nodded gratefully.

'Then I asked him not to drop you for
today. That today would be your last game.
As a favour to me.'

James looked into his dad's eyes. His dad
looked sad. It was his dream to see his son do

what he had done. But, all the same, he wasn't forcing James to do anything. He was respecting his son's choice.

'Thanks,' James said again.

'And your mum's coming down to see it too.'

James smiled, then saw his dad turn and nod at Steve.

An Announcement

S teve looked out across the canteen,
watching the boys slurping from
bowls, stuffing toast into their mouths,
drinking three kinds of fruit juice all mixed
into one.

'Today,' Steve said, 'is going to be a
long day. I wanted to run through it with
you.'

The team and the other adults all stopped
eating and talking. They were – as usual –
quiet for Steve. And people wanted to know

what was going to happen today. But also what was going on.

'We leave in an hour for West Ham. There's thirty minutes or so for some light training once we're there. Then we watch the losers' final.'

A cheer spread quickly through the canteen. Steve grinned, then put his hand out to silence the lads.

'Then it's us and Chelsea. The final.'

Another cheer.

'After that,' Steve said, 'we come back here. And we *stay* here.'

There were a couple of muted laughs. Somehow Steve had created a good atmosphere, even after the news about sending two lads home.

'And tonight,' Steve said, 'we're going to be having a party.'

This time the cheer was louder. A couple of chairs fell over.

'We've food and drink. And . . .' Steve did a drum roll on the table. '. . . a karaoke competition.'

The next noise the lads made was half cheer, half groan.

Once it had gone quiet, Steve held his hand out again. 'There's one more announcement.'

He looked over at James. James nodded.

'Today is James's last game for United.'

Several voices spoke at once.

'What?'

'Why?'

'No way.'

'Is he signing for West Ham?'

Everyone was looking at James.

'James,' Steve said, 'is going to move on and do other things. He is *not* signing for West Ham!' He paused again. 'James has been a great player for United. I've worked with him for a few years and I'll miss him. As a player, but mostly as a good lad.'

A round of applause echoed round the canteen. James smiled, then put his head down.

'Today,' Steve went on, 'is going to be a tough game. But I think we're going to play well. This is James's last game. So shall we win it for him?'

The cheer that went up this time was deafening.

Chelsea v United

A large crowd had gathered for the game. There must have been over four hundred people along one side of the pitch and behind the goals.

And the Chelsea team were big. Very tall for eleven-year-olds.

Steve gathered the United team together into a huddle.

'So, we've talked about this. They're big lads. We saw how they beat West Ham. They're not playing long ball, but they do put a lot of crosses into the box. And they do it early, so we have to be on our guard.'

The team nodded. James felt that there was a good team spirit. He really believed that they could win this.

'So we hold on to possession. We pass the ball about. We try to keep it down. We're not going to win a lot in the air. OK?'

Twelve voices said 'OK' back at the same time.

Steve grinned. 'Good lads. Let's do it then.'

Steve had been right about how Chelsea would play: they fired dozens of crosses into the box in the first half. It was an aerial assault.

But Tomasz was having a brilliant game. Every time a cross came in he'd be there, either grabbing the ball and holding it to his chest or punching it out of danger. And when

United managed to get the ball, they did well, pushing Chelsea back.

Jake was working really hard on the left wing. And the right back – who was supposed to be marking him – was struggling to stop his runs.

The best chance in the first half for United came after twenty-three minutes. Ryan passed the ball ahead of Jake. Jake ran on to it, then played a quick one-two with Chi. That left Jake time and space to cross the ball into Yunis on the near post.

Yunis couldn't reach it, but Will could. His header slammed against the crossbar and out for a goal-kick.

Steve was bubbling at half-time.

'Great stuff, lads. We're matching them. Just keep doing what you're doing and we've got a chance to win this.'

Ryan looked over at the Chelsea team. Most of them were sitting down.

'They're tired,' Steve said. 'If we can hold them off for another forty-five minutes, it's ours.'

The rest of the team put their hands together in the centre of the huddle.

'For James,' Ryan said.

'For James!' the rest of the team shouted out.

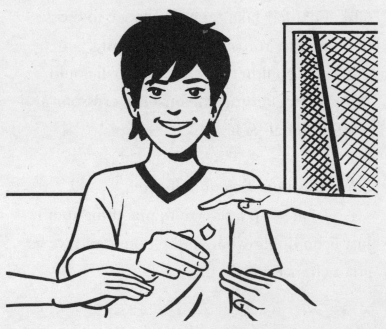

And the whole United under-twelves team cheered at the same time. Ready for the challenge.

One–Nil

United's under-twelves went on to the pitch feeling confident, strong and fit. And only a minute into the second half, Ryan found Jake with another pass. Jake made to run down the wing, hoping Yunis would be there for him on the near post. But, as he drew his leg back to cross the ball, he was tackled superbly. The Chelsea player who had tackled him gathered the ball and passed it to his team-mate, who launched it up the pitch.

Suddenly it was four against two. Four players in blue were sprinting towards James and Connor. And with a couple of passes they had cut both defenders out of the game.

Now it was down to Tomasz and his goalkeeping skills.

As the Chelsea striker brought the ball towards him, Tomasz ran out of his goal to narrow the angles and smother the shot.

But there was no shot to smother.

The ball was sailing over Tomasz. A perfect chip into the net.

One–nil to Chelsea.

The way the Chelsea players celebrated was hard to take. And even worse was the way the crowd of four hundred celebrated: they were mostly Chelsea fans.

United trudged back to their positions. They were losing.

But Ryan was in among them.

'Come on, we can do this. Remember, they're tired,' he said to the defenders and then to the midfielders. He was trying to fire the players up. 'We can be the first non-London team to win it,' he said. 'Do you want that?'

Once the game had settled down after the goal, the United players seemed more positive. Soon they looked more like a team that had just scored, not let one in. And

Chelsea were playing deeper, defending. Thinking they could win it now by just keeping United out.

And that's what happened.

United attacked and attacked for half an hour. Everything they tried failed. Jake couldn't find the space to run down the left because the right-sided defender *and* midfielder were barely leaving their half. And as much as Chi and Ryan tried to pass the ball up the middle, they couldn't get through.

There were ten minutes to go.

James glanced over at Steve. He looked frustrated and James knew why. There were no substitutes, no fresh legs. No Craig or Daniel. And Tony – the only other player left – had been injured against Arsenal the day before.

James wanted to start playing long balls into the Chelsea area, but he remembered both Steve and Ryan had said they should

stick to their plan: keep playing the ball along the ground, keep passing.

Two minutes later it worked.

Chi collected the ball in the centre circle. He played it to Jake. But instead of running with the ball, Jake did something different. He drew the Chelsea defenders and midfielders towards him and suddenly drove the ball across the width of the pitch to Ben, who was unmarked on the far right.

Ben ran towards the penalty area fast. Very fast.

Jake's pass had turned Chelsea inside out.

No one had got to Ben by the time he reached the edge of the area. Ben had two players to pass to: Will and Yunis, two strikers hungry for a touch of the ball. But Ben passed to neither of them.

He shot.

A low hard shot that rocketed past three defenders and the Chelsea keeper before they had seen it.

Goal.

The crowd had gone quiet. But slowly, after a few seconds, they began to applaud Ben.

Ben smiled. He looked over at Steve, who was clapping too.

One–one.

After congratulating Ben, Ryan came over to Jake.

'Great cross, Jake.'

'Cheers.'

'Now you'll have some space to play in. Attack them.'

Jake put his thumb up. 'I will,' he said.

Two Minutes

Ryan was right about the game opening up. Jake had loads more space now.

With two minutes to go, Jake took a great pass from Chi. It left Chelsea stretched. Jake touched the ball twice and found himself on the edge of the penalty area.

He had three options.

Pass it into the path of Ben on the far side of the pitch?

Hold the ball up and wait for Yunis and Will to get into the penalty area?

Or shoot?

Without thinking any more, Jake shot.

The ball powered across the face of the goal, past the keeper, towards the top corner of the net. But, just as it looked like it was going to be a goal, a Chelsea defender made it back. He managed to get his head on to the ball and deflect it over the bar.

Corner.

Ben waited patiently for the crowd to return the ball. Eventually they did. They were quieter now that United were back in the game.

Ben lined the corner up.

Jake watched him. He looked nervous with so many people standing near him.

Ryan was calling extra players forward.

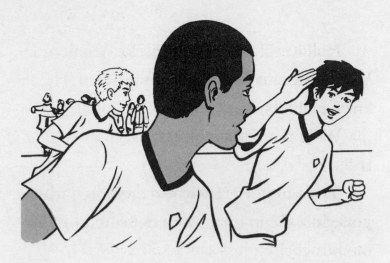

He knew this was the last chance they had to win the game in normal time.

'James,' he shouted. 'Come up. You too, Connor.'

The ball came sailing over the penalty area. Ben had over-hit it. But Jake was waiting on the left. He trapped the ball and lofted it back into the six-yard box. The Chelsea players had started to move out of the area, maybe trying to get the United forwards offside.

But not quickly enough.

As the ball sailed towards the penalty area, James made a short run forward. He knew he had a minute left as a United player. This could be his last touch of the ball.

James jumped. Like he'd seen his dad jump in the cup final when he scored his famous goal.

James met the ball with his head. It rocketed towards the net. The keeper got his hand on to it to push it over the bar for another corner, but it was too powerful.

The ball was in.

Goal.

Two—one.

James was aware of three things when his team-mates leaped on his back.

His mum and dad grinning on the touchline.

The Chelsea players slumped, some kneeling, defeated.

And the hundreds of watching fans applauding.

Applauding James's last goal for United.

There was a short ceremony at the end of the game. There were winners' and losers' medals and the presentation of the Christmas Cup.

Lots of the fans stayed on for the awards, plus the four teams.

After United had collected their medals, Ryan turned to James. 'You go and collect the trophy, James,' he said.

'I can't,' James said. '*You're* the captain.'

'Please,' Ryan said. 'Go on. It's your last chance.'

'But I shouldn't. You should.'

'You scored the winner,' Ryan said.

James smiled. 'OK,' he said. 'Thanks, Ryan.' Then he looked over at his dad.

And so, standing a few yards away, Cyril Cunningham, former West Ham and England player, saw his son step up to collect a football trophy for the first – and last – time.

He smiled, joining in the applause.

Thursday 22 December
Chelsea 1 United 2
Goals: Ben, James
Bookings: none

Under-twelves manager's marks out of ten for each player:

Tomasz	8
Connor	7
James	10
Ryan	9
Ronan	7
Chi	6
Sam	6
Jake	8
Yunis	7
Will	7
Ben	9

Karaoke

Back at the accommodation, the whole team had gathered for the Christmas party. There were streamers across the canteen, balloons and lots of food.

And the Christmas Cup was sitting – pride of place – on the main table.

Secret Santa presents had been received. Jake had got Ryan a United scarf. Yunis presented Steve with a Superman mug. And Ryan gave Tomasz a football story, but one that had been translated into Polish.

Tomasz beat James's dad in the *FIFA 10* final, though most people reckoned the former England international let him win.

As Steve had promised, the party finished with karaoke. Most of the lads did famous Christmas songs, with mixed results. Steve and Will's mum sang a duet of a song called 'Little Drummer Boy'.

Everyone was laughing and enjoying themselves. Chi had made up a scoreboard to

score each song. Steve and Will's mum got nines. Ryan and Ben got fives for singing 'Rudolph the Red-Nosed Reindeer'.

Then, eventually, it was James's turn. He took the microphone from Steve, suddenly looking nervous.

The room went silent.

And then James began to sing.

The atmosphere in the room was different from how it had been for the other songs. This time it was serious. The boys had stopped laughing and making fun. They were listening.

James was singing like a real singer. It was amazing.

And the team soon realized who the song was for. It was James singing to his mum and dad. After all that had happened over the last few days, he was singing a song for his parents.

Will's mum listened. She was smiling.

At the end of the song there was silence for a moment. Then Chi put up his board.

Ten.

'That was wonderful,' Will's mum said.

James smiled. 'Thanks,' he said.

Then he felt his dad's arms come around him in a huge bear-hug. And his mum too.

FIFA 10 **Final scores**

James's dad	5–7	Tomasz

Father to Son

'That was brilliant,' Dad said. 'I never knew . . . You were excellent. This is what it's all about, isn't it?'

James smiled. He hadn't even needed to tell his dad what he wanted to do instead of football. His dad had guessed it straight away.

'Thanks,' he said.

'Did you ever talk to your mum about wanting to be a singer?' Dad asked, glancing over at his wife.

'No. But . . .'

'. . . but *she* knew?' Dad finished his sentence.

'She knew something was up.'

The party was going again now. Loud voices were calling out and someone else was singing.

'Why didn't you talk to us about it?' Dad said.

'I didn't want to upset you. Because I know football means so much.'

Dad nodded.

'And when we went to West Ham,' James said, 'and all those mates of yours were telling me I was going to lift a trophy like *you* did that day . . .' James paused. 'Well, it did my head in.'

Dad smiled. 'I know,' he said.

They were silent for a minute.

'How did you feel about playing your last game?' Dad asked.

James grinned. 'Good,' he said.

James thought his dad was going to say
something, but he just breathed out.

'Do you understand why I want to give
football up?' James asked.

'To sing?' Dad shook his head. 'No,
James. Not really. But I respect it. It's your
choice.'

'I like football. But I don't want it to be
my life,' James said. 'Like when you were

saying I'd have to be more involved once I'm fifteen. I just don't want to.'

'I understand that,' Dad said. 'It was my life for twenty years. Football. Football. Football. But that was before you were born.'

'I want to do singing,' said James. 'At school they think I've got a chance.'

'A chance of what?'

'Of becoming a real singer – for a job. I could go to that music college in town. I love it, Dad. I know it's stupid – wanting to sing – but I –'

'Who said it was stupid?' Dad demanded. He sounded angry.

'It just is,' James said. 'Football's cool. Skateboarding is cool. PSPs are cool. But singing?'

'Singing is brilliant,' Dad said. 'And I'm really proud you've found something you love.'

James smiled. His dad supported him and he couldn't believe it. He wished he'd told him about it weeks ago.

Thank Yous

Thank you, as always, to my wife, Rebecca, and daughter, Iris, for their ongoing support and encouragement with my books. And to Rebecca in particular for reading it at its various stages and giving me such unflinching and intelligent advice.

Thanks to Ralph Newbrook and Jim Sells for their football advice.

And to Sophie Hannah and James Nash for excellent feedback on the novel in its first draft.

Thanks, as always, to Burnley FC for allowing me to spend time at their training ground and get some of the facts about academy football straight.

And to Nikki Woodman for reading it through and giving me great feedback.

Thanks to the football writers' group. And to Thomas Wigg for introducing me to the PSP.

The Football Academy series came about thanks to the imagination and hard work of Sarah Hughes, Alison Dougal and Helen Levene at Puffin, working with David Luxton at Luxton Harris Literary Agency. Thanks are due to all four for giving me this opportunity. Thanks also to Wendy Tse for all her hard work with the fine detail, and to everyone at Puffin for all they do, including Reetu Kabra, Adele Minchin, Louise Heskett, Sarah Kettle and Tom Sanderson and the rights team. And thanks to Brian Williamson for the great cover image and illustrations.

Bright and shiny and sizzling with fun stuff ...

puffin.co.uk

WEB CHAT

Discover something new
EVERY month – books, competitions and treats galore

WEB NEWS

The **Puffin Blog** is packed with posts and photos from Puffin HQ and special guest bloggers. You can also sign up to our monthly newsletter **Puffin Beak Speak**

WEB FUN

Take a sneaky peek around your favourite **author's studio**, tune in to the **podcast, download activities** and much more

WEBBED FEET

(Puffins have funny little feet and brightly coloured beaks)

Point your mouse our way today!

It all started with a Scarecrow

Puffin is well over sixty years old.
Sounds ancient, doesn't it? But Puffin has never been
so lively. We're always on the lookout for the next big
idea, which is how it began all those years ago.

Penguin Books was a big idea from the mind of
a man called Allen Lane, who in 1935 invented
the quality paperback and changed the world.
**And from great Penguins, great Puffins grew,
changing the face of children's books forever.**

The first four Puffin Picture Books were hatched in 1940 and the
first Puffin story book featured a man with broomstick arms called
Worzel Gummidge. In 1967 Kaye Webb, Puffin Editor, started the
Puffin Club, promising to **'make children into readers'.**
She kept that promise and over 200,000 children became
devoted Puffineers through their quarterly instalments of
Puffin Post, which is now back for a new generation.

Many years from now, we hope you'll look back and
remember Puffin with a smile. **No matter what your age
or what you're into, there's a Puffin for everyone.**
The possibilities are endless, but one thing is for sure:
whether it's a picture book or a paperback, a sticker book
or a hardback, **if it's got that little Puffin
on it – it's bound to be good.**